Chippiepierre's Magic Paintbrush Tail
A Steamboat Adventure

Barbara Dietz

Illustrations by George Frayne

Chippiepierre's Magic Paint Brush Tail: A Steamboat Adventure
Copyright © 2013 by Barbara Dietz

Published by Merry Point Press
P.O. Box 163
Merry Point, Virginia 22513

Illustrations by George Frayne

Original oil painting of steamboat Lancaster
© 2013 Richard Kantor
All rights reserved.

ISBN-10: 1-49128-194-4

Book Design by Tom Crockett; tomcrockett@mac.com

To order additional copies contact the author at www.barbaradietz.com
or by email at riverb@nnwifi.com.

Chippiepierre's Magic Paintbrush Tail
A Steamboat Adventure

Barbara Dietz

Illustrations by

George Frayne

Merry Point, Virginia,
2013

Dedication

To my husband Richard,

the love of my life and a great cat dad.

And to my mom,

thank you for everything.

Original Oil Painting of Steamboat Lancaster
Richard Kantor.

To order prints of the Steamboat Lancaster or to view other artwork by Richard Kantor
visit chesapeakeartbyrichardkantor.com.

Introduction
Steamboat Travel: Why Was It Important?

My hope is that this adventure with Chippiepierre, Gidgett, and Captain Tom entertains children while teaching them about the Steamboat Era on Chesapeake Bay. This unique time in the tidewater region of Virginia and Maryland is not well represented in children's books.

In the 1800's and into the early 1900's steamboats plied navigable waterways throughout the country transporting passengers and cargo.

On the Chesapeake Bay's rivers, and tributaries steamboats played a vital role. Overland travel by horse or wagon was often difficult, if not impossible. There were few roads and their conditions were poor. In some areas railroads did not exist. In the rural tidewater region of Virginia and Maryland, steamboats linked people from rural areas to the cities of Baltimore and Norfolk and to small towns in between.

Life along the water was synchronized with the steamboat schedules. As the steamboat's whistle blew the wharf would come to life, as farmers and watermen prepared to transport their livestock and harvests for sale in Baltimore. Passengers would anxiously wait to board the steamer for their journey as others would disembark. People not traveling on the steamboat would come down to the wharf to see all the activity, while others would place their orders for goods with the ship's purser. The items would then be delivered on a return trip.

This way of life played out for over 100 years. Slowly, the use of automobiles and trucks for transporting goods, along with improved roads, diminished the need to travel by steamboat. In 1933, a major hurricane swept up the Chesapeake Bay damaging many of the wharfs beyond repair. In 1937, following a fatal fire on one of the steamers, new safety regulations were enacted affecting the economic viability of running a steamboat line. These factors ultimately resulted in the demise of the golden age of steamboat travel.

Chippiepierre's Journey

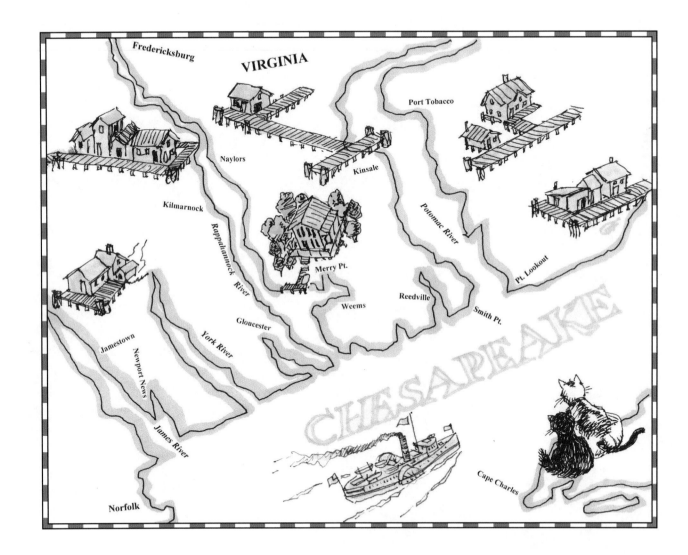

x

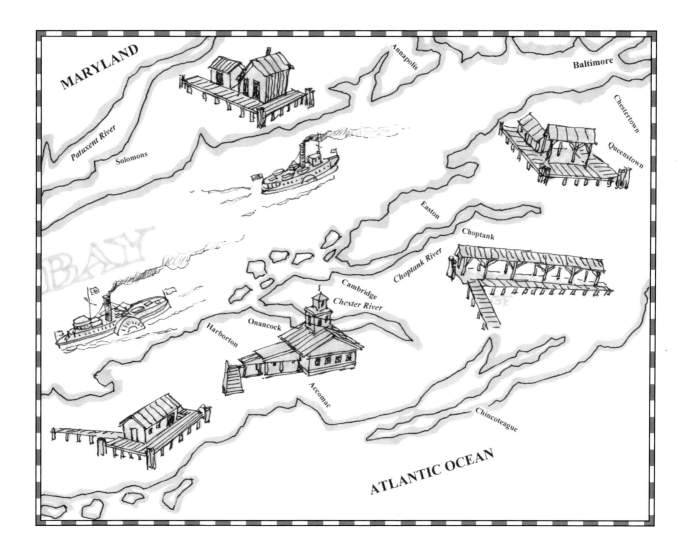

Chapter One
Chippiepierre's Secret

Chippiepierre bounded down the basement stairs two at a time. It was still very early in the morning and no one else in the house was awake.

"I hope the painting is something fun," he said, as he neared the basement door. He entered the basement and the familiar cool air mixed with the smell of Windsor Newton oil paints and mineral spirits filled the room. His beautiful white and black fur coat glimmered, as the morning sun poured through the windows. His tail was long and all black. The black spot on the top of his head was tilted so it just touched the bottom of his left ear, like a beret, the kind French artists wear. He was a very tidy, proper, large, athletic cat.

"I just have to see what he was painting last night, I won't hurt anything by looking," Chippiepierre thought. With ease, he jumped up on the work table.

"I will be very quiet and no one will learn my secret."

From the table, he had a better view of the painting on the easel. "It's a big boat, but not like anything I have ever seen in Davis Creek or on the Corrotoman River. What's that big wheel on the side?"

Chippiepierre studied the painting a bit more closely, and slowly spelling out each letter on the side of the boat he put the word together. "L-a-n-c-a-s-t-e-r," that must be the name of this boat."

"PURRRR meooow?"

"Gidgett! You scared me! Don't you know you aren't supposed to sneak up like that?"

"Sorry, I didn't mean to scare you."

Gidgett's long black fur also glistened. Her fluffy tail was at least as big as she was. Her four white paws looked like dainty white dress-up gloves, like ladies wear to church sometimes. On either side of her face, brown highlights showed through her long mane. Her bright, yellowish- green eyes were perfectly round.

"Whatja doing down here?" Gidgett asked.

"Uhh, me? Nnnnnothing really," stammered Chippiepierre, not wanting to divulge his secret or arouse Gidgett's curiosity.

"Can I do nothing with you?" asked Gidgett, as she pawed at a foam ball and playfully pushed it across the floor.

"No! Can't you see I'm busy?"

"I thought you said you weren't doing anything," answered Gidgett quickly.

"What I mean is, it isn't anything you'd be interested in."

"Why does she always have to ask so many questions?" thought Chippiepierre, knowing it was going to be very hard to get her to go back upstairs and leave him alone.

"It looks to me like you are bothering all the paint supplies on the work table. You know you aren't supposed to get up on that table, or anywhere near a painting on the easel."

The painting was shiny because the fresh oil paint had not dried from last night's work.

"I'm ....not bothering anything, I am just admiring the painting, that's all. Now why don't you go back upstairs? Do I hear kitchen sounds? You don't want to miss breakfast. I'll be right up." Chippiepierre knew he didn't hear anything, but he hoped that he could trick Gidgett into going upstairs.

Gidgett didn't budge. Instead, she watched Chippiepierre, who was in a trance, as he focused on the many tubes of paint on the table, the colorful blobs of paint on the pallette, and the painting on a large oval canvas that was carefully secured to the easel. He didn't understand the mysterious names of the paints, like Crimson or Viridian, but he loved the richness of the colors and the magical effect when two or more colors were blended together.

He stared longingly at the painting. He was carefully balancing himself between the easel and the table. He wanted very badly to add a bit more color.

"Maybe just a bit more yellow in the sky," he said, forgetting that Gidgett was still in the room, "and perhaps a dab more blue in the water."

Gidgett watched from the floor in wide-eyed disbelief, as Chippiepierre touched his tail first to a blob of yellow paint on the palette and then to the canvas. Then he did it again and again, carefully adding colors to the painting like a real artist. She couldn't believe her eyes as the tip of his black tail was transformed into a paintbrush, and the black spot on his head magically became an actual beret.

"Chippiepierre! What's that thing on your head? Your black spot, it's become a hat! Your tail, it's a paintbrush! What's happening to you? You'll get us in trouble for touching that painting!"

Startled out of his trance, Chippiepierre lost his balance. He tried to catch himself on the table ledge, but in a panic, he reached out and clawed onto the easel. The whole easel rocked. The boat in the painting was rocking like a boat on a stormy sea, and then… CRASH, BAM, BOOM!

Chapter Two
A Very Different Place

A wooden floor was rocking under him, and it was hard to stand up on all four paws without swaying. It gave him a sick feeling.

"What happened, and where am I? It's so dark. What's all that noise? Why do I hear water splashing?"

There was a sliver of light seeping into the darkness, so he moved cautiously towards the light and peeked out.

"Look at all the people. Who are they? They are dressed so differently, and what is that splashing sound?" As he peered out from his hiding place, he could hear the sound of seagulls overhead, and with his especially sensitive sniffy nose, he detected many unfamiliar smells mixed with salty air. Just a few feet away was a very large line, neatly coiled. "That line would be way too heavy for a string game," thought Chippiepierre, as he pictured the bathrobe belts and strings he was familiar with in his toy basket. Chasing a string was always a favorite game of his. His people would pull a string around obstacles in the house, and he would give chase. Sometimes, he would catch it and pull it away. "That rope is way too big, and besides, no one is even pulling it around. Gidgett always prefers to play with a ball; she says you can push it around on your own. And you don't really need anyone else to play. It's even better to bounce it down the stairs and race it to the bottom."

"GIDGETT!!! Oh my gosh! Where is she?" thought Chippiepierre, remembering the painting crashing to the basement floor. "I bet I'm on a boat like the one in the painting with the big wheel on the side. What was that boat's name? I have to think. Was it The Land Keeper? No, that's not it. Was it The Land Skipper? Nope, that's wrong. I know. It was The Lancaster. That's it!" Chippiepierre was frightened. His fur stood up on his back, and his tail swelled to twice its usual size.

"What will I do? Is Gidgett here? She was standing beneath the easel when the painting fell. If I'm here,

she could be here, too. I have to find her, but I don't know how or even where to begin looking." He cautiously slipped out from under a life boat stored on the ship's deck. Filled with fear and doubt, he slinked along the boat's deck, staying hidden in the shadows, which was one of his best skills.

"What would the people on board this ship do if they saw me?" He shuddered at the thought. There was lots of noise, with men and women strolling and talking. Workers were moving large crates, barrels, sacks, steamer trunks, and suitcases.

"It's almost like a little town, but on the water, yet everything seems different than at home." He slithered under railings and jumped up and over boxes. As he made his way, the sloshing, splashing, and churning sound grew louder. Chippiepierre jumped up, balanced on a nearby hand railing, and peered overboard into the dark blue swirling water.

"Oh my gosh! I AM on that boat in the painting, and IT'S MOVING! Where am I going?" A big box on the side of the boat held a large paddle-wheel, churning through the water pushing the boat forward. The movement of the boat made it hard for him to keep his balance on the narrow railing. Balance usually came quite naturally to Chippiepierre.

"I have definitely never seen a boat like this before. That wheel is enormous, and the water looks deep. If I fell in, how would I get out?" That thought caused Chippiepierre's tail to puff up, and he swiftly jumped off the railing to the safety of the boat's deck. He shook his head several times to lose the scary thought of falling overboard.

"I must find Gidgett, and we must go home. By now our people will be awake and having breakfast. They will be filling our bowls and wondering where we are." His mind drifted back home. Every morning he would wait for his loving people to awaken. Sometimes he would help them wake up with gentle nuzzling and purring. Then he would lead them to the kitchen and roll under their feet, while his and Gidgett's bowls were filled.

"Breakfast is my favorite meal of the day, and I'm hungry. That's it! There must be a kitchen on this boat and with any luck that's where I'll find Gidgett; or at least a little breakfast." Chippiepierre tilted his head, nose-up, to sniff at the air until he zeroed in on the aroma of food.

"M-m-m - yes indeed, this is the way to the kitchen."

Chapter Three
The Narrow Escape

"This boat is much bigger than any I have ever seen before. There are so many people on it; I wonder where we could be going?" As he rounded a corner the smell of breakfast filled the air. People were lined up waiting to go through the door, and occasionally someone or a group of people would come out.

"That's it! There must be breakfast happening behind that door. That's where I'll find Gidgett. I just know she's in there, she never misses a meal. How can I get through the door without being seen?" Chippiepierre stayed in the shadows near the doorway and studied the people coming and going, plotting a way to get in.

"The people are dressed very differently here, than at home. The men are all wearing hats and suits, and the ladies have big frilly dresses that flare at the bottom and touch the floor. They certainly are all dressed up."

Suddenly, he had a plan, but his timing would have to be perfect. He waited for the perfect moment to make his move. He waited as people went in and out the door. The smell of breakfast would have caused another cat to act too quickly, but not Chippiepierre. He could be very patient. As hungry and desperate as he was to find Gidgett, he had to execute his plan with precision.

Then it happened. A lady wearing a long dress, ruffled and flared at the bottom, approached the door from the side where he was waiting. The lady was also carrying a fancy umbrella, which he thought odd since it wasn't raining. There was a small step just in front of the door. As the lady gently lifted the bottom of her dress to clear the step, Chippiepierre slipped underneath and walked through the door undetected.

He had to walk very carefully as the lady and her friend were escorted to a table. He could not see where they were going from underneath the dress and did not want to be seen. Once the couple was seated Chippiepierre peered carefully out from underneath the table and the sea of ruffles.

"Oh no!" he gasped, as he looked out from under the table. "This is not the kitchen. Look at this fancy room."

It was a beautiful dining room with green leather chairs and rich, warm wood paneling. All around him people were seated at tables and eating breakfast. It all smelled so good.

"I am trapped in the middle of this dining room, how will I ever find the kitchen? If only I hadn't touched the painting this morning, I wouldn't be here now." Chippiepierre was feeling lonely, scared, hungry, and homesick all at once. As he pondered his situation, he thought of all the other times he had traveled into paintings. The subjects of those paintings were of familiar surroundings: the creek he and his family lived on; the flower garden at the end of the lane; even the big river. He had traveled into those paintings and been able to get home because he knew where he was. On those art adventures, he just simply walked home.

"This time it's all different. Everyone is all dressed up; this boat is like something I've never seen before; I don't know where I'm going and worst of all, Gidgett probably fell into this painting with me."

Then it dawned on Chippiepierre. "Maybe the ladies are wearing long fancy dresses, carrying umbrellas and the men are wearing suits because this is the way things were in the past. OH MY GOSH! Could we have traveled back in time? That could explain why this boat has two giant side-wheels. Oh, we are really very lost."

Chippiepierre was startled out of his thoughts when he heard the lady excuse herself from the table.

"Uh oh, if she's getting up, I must go with her." So he walked through the dining room under cover of the dress, being careful to stay amongst the ruffles but not accidentally rub against the woman's legs. He was very experienced in the art of avoiding feet, especially at mealtime. Back home, he would mill around in the kitchen, near his people's feet, just close enough as a reminder it was feeding time. Very rarely did his method ever fail him.

As he made his way across the room, under cover of his escort's ruffled dress, someone shouted from across the dining room, "SNAKE! Madam!

There's a snake under your dress!" The scream was so loud it startled all the passengers in the dining room. Chippiepierre froze with fear.

"I'm afraid of snakes, where is it?" He thought, as he stayed amongst the ruffles, trying desperately not to move and give himself away. He could hear a lot of commotion and he sensed the threat was very close and getting closer. Suddenly, he realized the "snake" was actually his long black tail sticking out from underneath the lady's dress. Chippiepierre couldn't help himself. He bolted out from under the ruffles and took off running full speed across the dining room, bells on his collar jingling all the way. A few people gave chase, while others laughed. He ran out of the dining room and down a flight of stairs. He came upon a pair of swinging doors. Timing the swinging doors perfectly, he ducked inside. Somehow his tail made it through.

Chapter Four
Captain Tom

From his new hiding place, under a marble-topped work table, pots and pans clanked and waiters ran in and out carrying large trays of delicious smelling food.

Chippiepierre was breathless and very hungry, but he kept still. What had happened in the dining room had likely sent people looking for him all over the ship.

The kitchen smells were overpowering.

"I am so hungry. If I just had a little something to eat, I could focus on finding Gidgett."

A table across the room was loaded with trays full of hot meals destined for the dining room.

"Should I take a chance and jump up on the table?" From his hiding place, he visually measured the distance and height of the table. He knew he could easily make the jump, as he was a tall and athletic cat.

"No… the risk of being seen is too great, and I've already caused enough trouble." He turned his attention away from the food on the table and scanned his surroundings. At first he thought it a mirage. Across the room just at cat height, in an out of the way corner on the floor, he spied two bowls.

"Well, those are pet bowls, and I am a pet. And I am hungry and thirsty. Whoever the owner is certainly won't mind if I have a small taste and a sip of milk." So, once again using his skill to avoid being stepped on, he carefully out maneuvered all the scurrying feet, made it safely to the bowls in the corner, and began to eat. He was so hungry that as he helped himself to food and milk he didn't even notice the big red tabby cat watching him.

"Ahoy there bud, this is MY galley! I didn't know we hired more crew."

Startled, Chippiepierre looked up,

milk still on his whiskers. The red tabby was big and muscular with more white stripes than Chippiepierre had ever seen on any cat before. His head was large and lopsided. The tip of his left ear was missing. His fur was weathered and very thick.

Chippiepierre, mesmerized by all the stripes, and taken aback by the red tabby's scruffy appearance, tried to speak up.

"Uhh, no, I'm not crew."

"Oh, I see. So you're a passenger. All passenger pets must be in their cabins. I'll need to see your ticket. Heading to Baltimore?"

"Uhh nnno," answered Chippiepierre nervously. "I don't have a ticket. I'm not really a passenger."

"Let me get this right. You are in my galley. You are eating my food. You have no ticket and you're not really a passenger. Well I'll be!" exclaimed the striped tabby. "You're a stowaway! We haven't had a stowaway in years. Let's hear your story, and it better be a good one. Then I'll have to make my report."

The red tabby carefully studied the stranger. He noted Chippiepierre's green and white checked collar with a shiny red heart-shaped tag, small bell and his overall tidiness. His fur was sleek and well-groomed. His ears were very clean with hints of pink that actually matched his moist pink nose. Most of all, he was puzzled by the hat on Chippiepierre's head. It was, he thought, a bit odd for a cat to wear a beret. It made him look like one of those French artists.

"You look more like one of those pampered city cats than you do a stowaway," said the red tabby, still eyeing Chippiepierre suspiciously.

"Me, a stowaway? It's… it's not like that at all," stammered Chippiepierre.

"Let's hear it then," said the red tabby impatiently but also intrigued.

"I am so hungry, and the food smells so good. I saw the bowls, and I have lost my friend. We fell into a painting because it needed a bit more yellow in the sky. Some people are chasing me because I caused a scene in the dining room, and I'm lost!" Chippiepierre trembled, exhausted and on the verge of tears.

"Slow down and get hold of yourself, mate. That is some story. Now, what's your name?"

"My name is Chippiepierre," he said trying to regain his composure.

"Is it now," said the red tabby, amused by the peculiar name. "I reckon you need a fancy name for that tag you're wearing. I guess you're some kind of fancy French city cat."

"Let me write this down for my report," said Captain Tom.

"C-H-I-P-P-I," the tabby struggled to write it down. "Can you spell that for me?"

Chippiepierre spelled slowly. "C-H-I-double-P-I-E-P-I-E double R-E." He had recited the spelling of his name many times and it all came easily to him; almost like a melody.

"Did you say two P's and one R?" asked the red tabby, frustrated with the spelling exercise.

"Actually, there are double P's then a single P and then double R's," answered Chippiepierre.

"Oh, never mind," said the spelling challenged tabby.

"Look Frenchy, my name is Captain Tom. I help run this steamship. So, it was you they were chasing. When I heard there was a cat that caused some trouble, I couldn't figure out what I'd done."

"Pleased to meet you," replied Chippiepierre, relieved that the conversation now seemed friendlier.

"Did you say you were looking for a friend?" asked Captain Tom.

"Oh yes! Have you seen her? She is much smaller than me with long black shiny fur, white paws, tummy and bib, and a humongous fluffy black tail. You see, at home there was a painting of this ship on the easel. I shouldn't have touched the painting, but I thought the sky needed a bit more yellow. And Gidgett, that's my friend's name, screamed and everything toppled over and here we are. Or at least this is where I think we are."

Captain Tom studied Chippiepierre for a moment while he pondered carefully what the newcomer had said. He noticed some small spots of yellow and blue paint on his fur, which seemed curious for such a well-groomed feline.

"Well, Frenchy, I don't know what to think of your tall tale about this ship being in some painting, but I think I do know where your friend is. Follow me."

Chippiepierre was so excited and relieved, that Captain Tom knew where Gidgett was, he raised his long black tail and began to purr his loudest purr, following the self-assured tabby close behind.

The ships' deck bustled with people and workmen. The two cats went down one flight of stairs and then another. It was very hot and very noisy. There was an unusually loud hissing. The further they went, the hotter it got, and the hissing grew louder and louder.

"It... sounds to me like there is a giant hissing cat down here," stammered Chippiepierre. "And it's so hot; maybe we shouldn't go any further."

"You want to find you friend, right?" asked Captain Tom.

"Y-y-yes, but the noise and the heat, is it safe?"

"The sound you hear is the ship's steam engine," explained Captain Tom. "Crews of men continually shovel coal into the furnace to keep the fire burning. Water is added to a big tank called a boiler to make steam. The steam drives the pistons that turn huge rods. The rods are attached to the walking beam which is attached to the side-wheels, and the ship makes way through the water."

Chippiepierre stared at the crew of shirtless men shoveling coal, feeding the furnace. Sweat dripped off the men covered in soot. He began licking at the sight of all the black coal, dust and grease. He thought, "They could all use a good tongue bath."

"Do those men like cats? Maybe they are still looking for me."

"Don't worry about those men, Frenchy. They are too busy to bother with you, and besides, it's too noisy down here. They couldn't possibly have heard what happened up on the main deck. Come on; I'll get you to your friend."

They passed through another set of doors and into a room loaded with all sorts of cargo in crates, barrels and trunks.

"There you go Frenchy"

Chippiepierre was puzzled.

"Where is Gidgett?"

"She's in that steamer trunk." answered Captain Tom.

"Which steamer trunk?" Chippiepierre asked impatiently. "There are all kinds of crates and containers in here. I don't even know what a steamer trunk is"

"People transport their belongings in them. She's in the one right in front of you," said Captain Tom.

"Well then, could you please get her out? Gidgett, are you in there?"

"Chippie, thank goodness you're here. Please help me. I can't get out and I'm scared. After the painting crashed I woke up on a bed in a little room with a lady I didn't know. The next thing I know she scooped me up and put me in this box. It's so dark in here."

There were small holes in the trunk. Chippiepierre peeked into the darkness and saw her yellow-green eyes glowing like headlights.

21

"Don't worry Gidgett; we'll get you out."

"Wait a minute, Frenchy. You just can't open that trunk and get her out. When she turned up in one of the ship's cabins, a nice lady passenger picked her up, figured she was lost and decided to take her home to Baltimore."

A sick feeling crept over Chippiepierre. Whatever Baltimore was, he didn't like the sound of it.

"No, no," shouted Chippiepierre. "I must get Gidgett out and she must come home with me to Merry Point. We already have a home. We can't go to Baltimore."

"Yes…"said Captain Tom suspiciously, "You need to get back into some painting that you both fell into. Are you sure you didn't take a spill and bump your head? Your story doesn't make much sense."

Chippiepierre was getting frustrated. "Look Mr. Tom or Mr. Captain or whoever you are, I really need your help. Won't you please help me get my friend out of this trunk before it's too late?"

"It's Captain Tom to you, Frenchy, and I suppose I can try to help. But we'll have to work fast, because this steamship will be pulling into Baltimore tomorrow night."

"Chippiepierre," Gidgett pleaded, from inside the trunk, "what's going on? I'm scared. Can you get me out? I don't think I want to go to Baltimore, whatever that is, and who is that with you?"

"We are trying to think of a way to get you out Gidgett. Please be patient, and I don't have time for formal introductions just now."

"I'm so hungry and I'm sorry I got us into this mess. I didn't mean to startle you, but I couldn't believe my eyes when you touched the painting and your tail turned into a paintbrush, and that beret grew on your head. I didn't want us to get in trouble, and I didn't even know you could paint."

Then she asked, "Where are we, anyway?"

"I think we are on the steamship in the painting, and I think we have traveled into the past." Chippiepierre whispered the last part softly, to avoid agitating Captain Tom. He realized Captain Tom was not receptive to the idea of traveling through paintings.

But Captain Tom did hear the discussion and interrupted. "You traveled into the past through a painting, indeed. I really should be reporting you. You're on the Steamship Lancaster, of the Weems Line, on the Chesapeake Bay heading to Baltimore. It is a two day trip. I could show you some charts. What more do you need to know?"

"Well," said Chippiepierre very timidly, almost afraid to ask, "What year is it?"

"You're kidding, right? How can you not know what year it is? It is 1894," said Captain Tom, shaking his head.

"1894!" gasped Chippiepierre. "We HAVE traveled back in time. What will we do?"

"Frenchy, I really don't have time to waste on this ridiculous notion of time travel, and falling in and out of paintings. Let's just concentrate on your friend for the moment. Perhaps once we get your friend out of this box we can have a reasonable conversation," said Captain Tom, shaking his head.

"You are right," said Chippiepierre. "There is no time to waste, let's come up with a plan."

"The trunk is heavy, and locked," observed Captain Tom. "I'm not sure how to break in."

 Chippiepierre approached the trunk, stood up on his hind legs and scratched furiously.

"Frenchy, you could scratch all day, but that trunk is locked and too strong to open that way.

It looks like we'll have to use gravity."

Chippiepierre was puzzled. "Okay, well then, let's get some of that, if you think it will work. Whatever it is, let's get some and let's get it quickly."

"Gravity is a physical force," explained Captain Tom. "It's what keeps things from floating into the sky. Do you know about, Sir Isaac Newton? "

"No," replied Chippiepierre. "I don't know any Mr. Newton, nor do I have time to meet him right now. I thought you said that you would help me get my friend out of this trunk."

"Frenchy, that's what I am talking about. The only thing I can think of

14

is to push the trunk over to those steps and let it tumble down. Hopefully it will break open, and your friend will be able to get out."

"Your plan is to push my friend down a flight of stairs?" gasped Chippiepierre.

"Yup, that's my plan," said Captain Tom calmly. "Besides, it is not a lot of steps and your friend will be just fine. Either that, or when the ship docks tomorrow night your friend goes to a new home in Baltimore. And what happens to you? I have no idea."

Chapter Five
Gravity

Once again Chippiepierre had a sick feeling. He realized that Captain Tom was probably right; maybe this was the only way to free Gidgett. Although he didn't like the idea, and he knew it was dangerous, he also knew time was running out.

"Gidgett," Chippiepierre shouted through the trunk, "It's going to be a little rough getting you out. Is there anything else in the box with you?"

"There is a blanket," answered Gidgett. "The lady put it in here with me."

"Great! Try to wrap yourself up in it, like you do at home in the laundry basket."

Gidgett knew exactly what he was referring to. She pictured herself at home. Warm laundry would be taken from the dryer and brought into the bedroom for sorting and folding. Gidgett would race into the bedroom, and in one leap she'd land in the pile and burrow as deep as she could into the soft warm laundry. Her people, would lovingly poke around to find her, tickling her little feet. She loved that game. For a moment, just thinking about it made her feel as if she was home. Then the darkness inside the box, closed in around her again.

"Chippie," Gidgett said softly, "I'm scared."

"Me too." whispered Chippiepierre.

"Okay Frenchy, let's try to push this trunk toward the stairs," said Captain Tom.

"On three; one... two... three!" Both cats stood up on their hind legs, and with their front paws leaned into the trunk. Chippiepierre pushed so hard it felt for a moment like the beret would pop right off of his head. All the white stripes in Captain Tom's red fur seemed to swirl around his muscular body. With all their effort, the trunk moved a little bit.

"Again!" shouted Captain Tom. And on the count of three, the trunk moved a bit more. Slowly they inched it towards the staircase, until it teetered on the very top stair. Chippiepierre was exhausted from pushing and frightened about what he would have to do next.

"Gidgett are you ready? Are you wrapped in the blanket?"

"Yes," her muffled voice replied, from inside the box.

Chippiepierre locked eyes with Captain Tom. They both knew what they had to do. Chippiepierre peered down the staircase. "These stairs look much steeper than when you first proposed the gravity method," said Chippiepierre.

"Let's just do this," said Captain Tom. "It will be over in seconds."

"I just hope it will be over in a good way," replied Chippiepierre.

He and Captain Tom both got behind the trunk one last time.

"One...two...three!" The box started to tumble down the stairs end over end. BANG, BUMP, THUMP all the way down. To Chippiepierre it seemed as though the trunk tumbled for an hour, but in seconds it hit the bottom. He and Captain Tom raced down the stairs.

"Gidgett, are you all right?" At first there was a silence. Then it was followed by a loud purring sound. It was Gidgett, as she squeezed through an opening in the trunk. Gidgett greeted Chippiepierre by licking his head right on his

beret, and he greeted his best friend by licking her face. They were so happy to be reunited, in the spirit of the moment; they gave Captain Tom a bunch of licks too.

Surprised at the affection, Captain Tom started to purr, which surprised him even more.

"Captain Tom, this is Gidgett. Gidgett, meet Captain Tom," said Chippiepierre, making sure to do proper introductions.

"You're all stripes!" exclaimed Gidgett, having never seen so many on one cat before. "And your fur is kind of messy. Are all those stripes hard to keep clean? What happened to your ear? You've got some kind of grease on you."

"Gidgett, that will be enough," admonished Chippiepierre. "Captain Tom is in charge of this ship, and he was nice enough to help get you out of that locked trunk. So what do you say, Gidgett?"

"Thank you, Captain Tom," said Gidgett, slightly embarrassed that Chippiepierre had to remind her of her of her manners.

"Well, you're welcome, I guess. Now I'd better be shoving off. It's time I got back to making my rounds," said Captain Tom. "I don't know what you are going to do now. We made a lot of noise and someone will be coming along to see what happened. Plus if that lady comes by to check on you and you aren't in the trunk, there could be trouble. I would lay low till the ship pulls into Baltimore. Don't cause any more trouble, or I will have to make a report. See you around." Captain Tom started to walk away.

"What? Wait!!" shouted Chippiepierre , "Don't leave us. We don't know where we are, and we need to get back home."

"I don't know anything about where all y'all came from, other than your tale about some painting, so I don't know how I could help," replied Captain Tom, still walking away.

"Didn't you tell me earlier that you could show us where we are?" asked Chippiepierre pleadingly. "You said something about a chart."

The desperation in Chippiepierre's voice grabbed at Captain Tom, he stopped and turned around. "There are charts and maps up in the Captain's quarters and pilot house."

"Please Captain, we really, really need your help," Gidgett said so sadly.

"Well, now that I have spent my morning on the both of you, I guess a little bit more time won't hurt anything. Besides, I reckon I wouldn't be fulfilling my duties if I let two strangers roam about the ship. Before we go topside, why don't you tell me one more time, slowly, where it is you are from. Maybe that will give me an idea how to help you get back home." Captain Tom was hopeful that Frenchy's story would make more sense. He hoped it would not include paintings and time travel.

"Didn't Chippiepierre tell you?" interrupted Gidgett. "Chippiepierre touched the painting that was on an easel in the basement of our home, and I screamed at him because he wasn't supposed to touch the painting. I didn't want him to get us in trouble. Then he grew a paintbrush tail and a beret, which caused him to knock the painting over, and here we are," explained Gidgett breathlessly.

"Yes…your friend Frenchy, here, did mention something about falling through a painting," said Captain Tom shaking his head. He realized this story was not going to go away and was surprised that Gidgett was verifying such a ridiculous tale. He also couldn't help noticing a few smears of paint on Gidgett.

"So, where do you live?" asked Captain Tom.

"In our house," answered Gidgett proudly.

"Gidgett, Captain Tom is asking specifically where we live," explained Chippiepierre.

"Our house is on Davis Creek just off the Corrotoman River, in Merry Point, Virginia," said Chippiepierre.

"Hmmm, the Corrotoman River you say?" inquired Captain Tom. "I know exactly where that is. The Corrotoman River flows into the Rappahannock, which flows into Chesapeake Bay. The Corrotoman is a fine little river. There are lots of tomato canneries there, plus crab and oyster packing houses. Merry Point is one of our regular stops. There's a post office and a well-stocked general store there. Yes, that's a fine little river; and a regular stop."

"Oh, goody!" exclaimed Chippiepierre. "You do know where we live. At the mouth of the Rappahannock there's a long narrow bridge. Does that sound familiar to you?"

"No, there are no bridges over the bay or rivers that I can think of, but there are ferries," answered Captain Tom.

Then it dawned on Chippiepierre that the bridge hadn't been built yet. That would be far into the future. As for the wharf, with a general store and post office, he knew they were no longer there, but he decided to keep that thought to himself.

For the first time since his adventure began, Chippiepierre was feeling a bit more confident that he and Gidgett would be able to get back home, since Captain Tom knew Merry Point. There was still the issue of time travel and how to get back to the right time, but it would be a start just to be in Merry Point.

"Okay Captain Tom, just let us know when we are getting near the wharf at Merry Point. When this ship pulls in and docks, Gidgett and I will make a run for it."

"Whoa, wait a minute there Frenchy. We've already done our run up the Rappahannock and Corrotoman Rivers, and we've rounded the Windmill Point light. We won't be back this way for two, maybe three days, depending on the schedule, which does change from time to time. Do you know of any other landmarks where you could possibly get off?"

"No, not really," said Chippiepierre. "Maybe if I could hear or see other names they might seem familiar."

"The names of the other wharfs will be on the charts up in the pilot house and Captain's Quarters. I guess we'd better go up there and let you look at the charts to see if you can recognize any other places along our route," said Captain Tom.

"I guess that's the best idea," said Chippiepierre hesitantly. "I'm only afraid that if we get off at a stop too far from Merry Point we won't recognize it and we'll still be lost."

Chapter Six
Off To The Captain's Quarters

The three felines set off to the pilot house and Captain's Quarters, which were on the top deck of the steamboat Lancaster. Captain Tom was familiar with life on the steamboat, but to Gidgett and Chippiepierre this was a strange place. Unsure of their surroundings, they scurried behind big packing crates, steamer trunks, barrels, and sacks of grain to stay out of sight. There was large equipment to jump over and under and there were smells that neither Chippiepierre nor Gidgett could identify. The din of noise put both cats on edge.

Chippiepierre hated loud noises; the scary sounds were distracting making it hard for him to keep an eye on Gidgett, while keeping up with Captain Tom. Finally, Captain Tom noticed that his new friends had fallen behind, so he ducked in between two large wooden barrels and waited for them to catch up.

"I would greatly appreciate it if you could go just a bit slower. We don't want to get separated or lost. Or should I say, more lost," said Chippiepierre, as he ducked in between the barrels with Captain Tom. They waited for Gidgett who was making her way slowly, sniffing the unfamiliar smells and pawing at the shadows that appeared and disappeared underneath all of the curious cargo.

"What is all this stuff, and where is it going?" asked Chippiepierre. He caught his breath and used the time to clean his paws and face, which were no longer snowy white, from climbing over and under things. He hoped that Captain Tom would take the hint and do some much needed grooming while waiting for Gidgett to catch up.

"This steamship carries oysters, crabs, fish, tools, crops, farm animals, farm equipment, mail, and passengers to wharfs up and down the Chesapeake Bay. Most wharfs have a general store and a passenger waiting area, plus areas for staging cargo and luggage. At each stop, cargo is loaded and unloaded, and passengers get on and off. Wait till you see how many people come down to greet the steamship when we pull in. It's really exciting, especially when the stevedores, those are the men that help load and unload the freight, and deck hands have to try to coax big farm animals up the loading gang plank. I have seen oxen push men right into the water. And just wait until you hear the ship's whistle."

Chippiepierre's mind was racing again as he half listened to Captain Tom. He couldn't share Captain Tom's enthusiasm for life on the steamship just now.

"With so many wharfs we will have to be careful not to get off at the wrong stop. We must keep going and get to the charts." said Chippiepierre.

"Come on Gidgett, you have to keep up. We have to look at the ship's charts and figure out where we are if we are ever going to find our way back home."

With those words, Gidgett became sullen and slumped down between Captain Tom and Chippiepierre. She was exhausted.

"Do you really think we can find our way back home?" asked Gidgett. "I miss our people; they are probably worried sick about us. If I was home right now I would be in one of their laps all curled up, and they would gently pet me. I am homesick, and I don't feel so good."

"Well," said Captain Tom, "it could be homesickness, but you're probably also seasick."

"Seasick?" they asked in unison.

"Yes, sometimes the rocking and rolling of the ship as she moves through the water can do that to you. Judging from the clouds and wind coming up it looks like some bad weather is heading our way. The water may get rougher, and the waves higher," explained Captain Tom.

Just as Captain Tom was going on about the weather, the clouds and the waves, all Gidgett could see was the horizon going up and down. The movement of the ship back and forth and up and down seemed magnified causing her to feel worse. Then it happened. She made a low heaving noise and threw up. Then she curled into a little ball, covered herself with her fluffy tail and meowed.

"Chippiepieere, I can't go any further, I am seasick, and so homesick."

The wind began to blow, and dark clouds enveloped the ship. The rain began with a few big fat drops, and with a loud clap of thunder the rain poured from the sky. Lightning flashed and snapped. The cats smelled electricity in the air. The thunder roared. The cats' watched as passengers and crew scurried to take cover.

"Come on!" ordered Captain Tom, "We can duck under this lifeboat to stay dry." Chippiepierre's tail swelled with fear with each bolt of lightning, and he nudged Gidgett to get her up.

"Get up Gidgett; you can rest under the boat."

The three new friends slipped under the lifeboat and peered out, watching and listening to the storm. The ship tossed in the rough water and

groaned under the strain. Water ran over the deck of the ship. Chippiepierre couldn't tell whether it was rain, or if waves were actually crashing over the deck. He wasn't certain he wanted to know. He cringed with each clap of thunder.

"When we have storms like this at home, we all go into the basement where it is safe and dry. I am always the first one in the basement at the first hint of thunder," Chippiepierre explained proudly.

"And the basement doesn't go up and down and make me seasick," added Gidgett, still feeling poorly.

"Neither of you have any sense of adventure," chided Captain Tom. "These storms are a part of life on a steamship. Every day is different, with so many places to go and people to meet. I have sailed on this ship my whole life, all over the Chesapeake Bay."

"Chippiepierre," Gidgett interrupted. "Can you remind me in the future that I do not like adventure? All I want is to be home with our people, food bowls, and toys, curled up in a warm sunbeam." Gidgett visualized her favorite spot on the bed, where the sun would shine in through the bedroom window each afternoon. Gidgett's wishful thinking caused Chippiepierre to think of his favorite place, the window seat on the second floor. From there, a safe vantage point, he would watch the birds and squirrels. For a moment Chippiepierre let out a soft purr just thinking about it. He knew every inch of the window seat. Suddenly, Chippiepierre was jolted out of his daydream by a flashing light piercing the
darkness of the storm.

"That light doesn't seem like a lightning bolt, but it sure is bright," said Chippiepierre, to Captain Tom. "It's a search light, isn't it? Somebody's determined to find us." With each flash, Chippiepierre flinched, and all his fur puffed out.

"Relax, Frenchy. That light is coming from the Smith Point lighthouse".

"There are houses on the water?" asked Chippiepierre, who when puzzled

tilted his head accentuating his beret.

"Like I said," replied Captain Tom, "There are many lighthouses on the Chesapeake Bay. There are four types of lighthouses: screwpile lighthouses, like Smith Point, look like houses built on stilts. Their light is on the roof; brick tower lighthouses are built on shore with a bright kerosene light on top; caisson's are tall towers built in the water; and integral lighthouses are basically houses built near the shore or on a bluff, with a light on the roof. They all flash light to act as a navigational guide for mariners. They warn the ship's captain and crew of points of land, and shallows so they don't run the ship aground. Each lighthouse flashes its light in a different pattern, and makes a different sound. The ship's captain can figure out where they are on the bay based on the lighthouse signals and fog horn. The captains' of these ships know the bay and the location of the lighthouses so well, they can determine their location and ship's speed by timing the distance between the lighthouses. In heavy fog it may be the only way to know their location."

"At home people use a GPS to find their location," said Chippiepierre.

"A GPS? What's that?" asked Captain Tom.

"Well," Chippiepierre said hesitantly, realizing that Captain Tom was probably not going to believe this either, "It stands for Global Positioning System. From any place on earth you can find your exact location. They are basically small computers that can pick up signals from satellites in space, orbiting the earth."

"Frenchy, computers, GPS, time travel, the next thing you'll be telling me is that men can fly," said Captain Tom shaking his head with a disapproving smirk.

Chippiepierre regretted mentioning the GPS system. To change the subject he said, "Look the sun is starting to come out, and the flashing from the lighthouse is fading. I'm glad it wasn't a searchlight."

.Me too," added Gidgett in agreement.

"Believe me Frenchy, the crew on this ship is much too busy to be chasing after two lost cats."

"That's reassuring but we don't want to take any chances."

"Gidgett, it is still lightly raining, but if you're feeling better we should get moving while the people are still inside," said Captain Tom. Gidgett was still wobbly but she got up and the three cats slipped out into a light drizzle.

"We have to go up to the very top deck," ordered Captain Tom. "The maps and charts are in the pilot house and Captain's quarters."

The three friends proceeded along the deck of the boat. They could hear the sound of the huge side wheels churning through the water. The water was still rough in the aftermath of the storm so walking was a little tricky, even for sure-footed cats on all fours. With each step Chippiepierre and Gidgett would lift each paw and shake the water off.

"At this rate it will take a month to get to the pilot house," grumbled Captain Tom. "A little water on the paws is no big deal. It isn't going to make you melt. Keep moving!"

"That's easy for you to say. But I have a lot of pride in my appearance." replied Gidgett, as she licked her paws and pulled at the wet and matted fur. "Once the paws are wet, things get caught and the fur can get sticky and ..."

"FRENCHY!" bellowed Captain Tom. "Do you want my help or not?"

"Of course we do," replied Chippiepierre in mid-lick.

"Then let's go!" ordered Captain Tom.

"Gidgett," whispered Chippiepierre, "Captain Tom is right. Let's keep moving; we can work on our fur later."

"We are heading up top-side," said Captain Tom pointing up at the very upper deck of the ship. "It's called the Hurricane Deck."

"I don't like the sound of that name," said Chippiepierre.

As Gidgett and Chippiepierre looked in the direction that Captain Tom was pointing, they both shouted, "Look a rainbow!"

"Let's make a wish," said Gidgett excitedly. "You can wish on a rainbow." So they both made a wish together. Neither one told the other what their wish was; they didn't have to.

"Frenchy! Gidgett! Double time!" shouted an irritated Captain Tom.

"Coming," they answered once again in unison.

43

Chapter Seven
Gidgett's Bright Idea

The three cats scampered along the deck and up a flight of stairs. As they made their way onto the hurricane deck Gidgett and Chippiepierre froze with fear. Their tails swelled; their backs arched, and their fur stood on end. In front of them, was the biggest spider they had ever seen. It would undoubtedly devour a small cat or two or even three. It was moving up and down and it looked like it was spewing black smoke into the sky. It was at least twenty feet tall.

"What is it now?" asked Captain Tom as he stared at the two paralyzed cats.

"Sssppidderrr," stammered Chippiepierre, almost unable to speak.

"It's a fire-breathing spider!" shrieked Gidgett.

"Oh, the walking beam. Relax. That's no spider," laughed Captain Tom.

"The walking what?" asked Chippiepierre still not taking his eyes off of the menacing structure.

"It's called a walking beam. It turns the big side wheels," explained Captain Tom. "Remember a while ago when I told you about the furnace and the boiler in the bottom of the ship that is fueled by coal, and how water is boiled to create steam which drives large pistons? Those pistons are attached to the walking beam. A huge crank is attached to the walking beam which turns the side wheels. That is what moves the ship. All of the smoke coming out of that smokestack behind the walking beam, is from the furnace."

"It still looks like a spider if you ask me," said Gidgett.

"It's scary," replied Chippiepierre cautiously.

"The whole operation of this steamship can be scary and very dangerous," explained Captain Tom. "Boilers and furnaces on other steamships have exploded; walking beams have crashed through the decking of ships and many a ship has run aground in the rivers and the bay. Fire is a real problem on these steamships because they are powered by huge coal furnaces. Many ships have burned right down to the water. We are almost to the pilot house and the Captain's Quarters. We have just one more small flight of stairs. Let's go."

Despite Captain Tom's reassurances, the two cats kept a watchful eye on the huge walking beam as they followed Captain Tom to the pilot house.

The three climbed the last flight of stairs and paused at the top. From the outside, the half-round pilot house seemed small compared to the rest of the ship. A small square building was attached.

"This is the Captain's Quarters." stated Captain Tom.

To Chippiepierre and Gidgett's surprise there was a small cat-sized door cut into the bigger door of the Captain's Quarters. It had brass hinges, and a polished name plate that read "CAPT. TOM."

"You live here in the Captain's Quarters?" asked Chippiepierre, now very impressed at the tabby's status on the ship.

"Of course, come aboard," said Captain Tom, as he pushed through the cat-sized door. Chippiepierre and Gidgett followed. As the door flapped shut, it barely missed catching Gidgett's fluffy tail.

The room seemed small and modest for the Captain of a ship. It had dark paneling, a bunk, a small dresser and a table with what looked to be charts or maps of some kind.

Chippiepierre was pleased how neat and orderly the little room was.

"Here you go, help yourselves," said Captain Tom.

"Help ourselves?" Chippiepierre shot back gruffly, or at least as gruffly as Chippiepierre could, which was not so much. "I thought you could help us. You said you could help us find our way home."

"I said I could show you the charts," corrected Captain Tom.

"Now let's take a look.

48

Here it is, Merry Point, right there."

Chippiepierre launched himself with ease up onto the table to see for himself.

"Okay, I see Merry Point. Please show me where we are now. These charts are a little confusing to read."

"Well, let's see," said Captain Tom studying the chart a bit more closely and figuring out loud. "About two hours ago we rounded Windmill Point. At twelve miles per hour, that's about 24 miles, subtract out a few miles per hour because of the chop during the storm. We saw the Smith Point Light. So I'd say we are just about right here," he said placing his sooty paw on the chart.

Chippiepierre moved in closely to look where Captain Tom was pointing and was momentarily distracted by the sooty paw, losing his train of thought. He shook his head to re-focus and looked at the chart. Nothing looked familiar.

"I must ask then, where is here?"

"Well," said Captain Tom, still pointing to the map, "that point of land is Point Lookout, Maryland. The next point of land will be Point-No-Point."

"I'll tell you what the point is," interrupted Gidgett impatiently. "The point is we have to get back home! We just have to go home NOW!"

Chippiepierre let out a deep sigh and hung his head.

"Maryland? We are so far from home, and the wheels on this ship keep pushing us farther and farther away. A lot of help this has been. All we know is that we are farther away from home than we thought we were."

Desperately, Chippiepierre looked directly at Captain Tom.

"Captain Tom, can you make them turn this ship around? After all, you're a Captain, right?"

"Now Frenchy, just how would I do that?"

"Well, since you're a Captain, use your Captainhood or Captainship. Order a change of course. Turn this ship around and take us back to Merry Point." Chippiepierre knew, even as he was saying the words, that it was unlikely that the red tabby had any such authority.

"Frenchy," said Captain Tom uncomfortably, "There are schedules that this ship must keep and besides….," Captain Tom's voice grew softer.

"Besides what?" shot back Chippiepierre sharply.

"Well, I'm more like a co-captain."

There was a long silence amongst the three cats. While they pondered their situation, Gidgett nervously licked her paws and touched them to her face and ears. Her long fur always needed extra grooming, and it helped to calm her and fill the awkward silence.

"I can't figure anything out. We are so far from home. All I can see is water. We may never be able to get back." The distress in Chippiepierre's voice alarmed Gidgett. She leaped up on the table with him and gently licked his beret. Licking soothed her, even if it was on Chippiepierre's beret.

"Well Frenchy, if you got here by falling through a painting, maybe you could fall back home through one, if that is really how you got here," said Captain Tom sarcastically.

"That is how we got here; why won't you believe us?" snapped Chippiepierre.

"It's just that most passengers get on and off the steamship by boarding at the different wharfs. There are many of these wharfs up and down the bay. People just don't fall onto the ship through paintings."

The heated exchange between Chippiepierre and Captain Tom made Gidgett nervous.

"Please stop arguing," pleaded Gidgett. "I have an idea."

"Well, I hope it's a good one because I am all out of ideas" said Chippiepierre, sullenly.

"Why don't you paint us home?"

"Paint us home?" Chippiepierre said, both puzzled and intrigued.

"Yes, like Captain Tom said. We got here by falling through a painting; let's fall back home through one. You could paint our home. Then we would just jump into it and we would be home."

Gidgett's words "we would be home" drained Chippiepierre's breath. He wanted desperately to be home with his people, on his sunny window seat overlooking his yard. Chippiepierre was so lost in his thoughts, that he didn't even notice Captain Tom exiting through the cat door. Instead, he tried to picture their home in as much detail as possible. He would need to paint all the details if he was going to paint them to the right home.

"Gidgett, you just might have the answer!" exclaimed Chippiepierre.

"I know you can do it," said Gidgett in her most supportive voice. "It isn't so different from what you've been doing at home, except this time you'll have to paint the whole picture from scratch."

Chippiepierre did not feel quite so confident. At home he had put many finishing touches on the paintings in the basement, and he enjoyed the smell of the paints and the turpentine. He had traveled into a few paintings upon touching them with his tail, but the subjects were local scenes. So, it was always easy to simply walk back home. He thought about the first time he added some touch-ups to a painting. It was a painting of the garden in the front of the house. He thought that the daffodils in the painting needed a touch more yellow. He carefully dipped his tail into the paint and touched it to the canvas. The next thing he knew he was out in the garden. When it happened, it startled him, but he just walked up on the porch and waited for the door to open to go back inside. He remembered his people being surprised when they opened the door and found him on the porch, waiting to come in. Later, when he reviewed his finishing touch, he thought it was perfect.

Painting a whole scene would be harder. Finishing touches were one thing, but a whole painting presented many challenges. He was afraid of where they could wind up if he couldn't paint a realistic picture of their home. He hadn't totally perfected the whole business of getting into the paintings. Sometimes it worked and other times it didn't. And this time it happened all by accident. This time he had to be sure to get them back to the right place in time with their people.

"Where is Captain Tom?" asked Chippiepierre, only just noticing the big red tabby was missing, and that he and Gidgett were alone in the Captain's Quarters.

"He went off to look for some paint supplies. He gave specific orders to wait here until he returned."

While they waited, Gidgett licked her fur quietly. Chippiepierre tried to visualize exactly what he would paint, every detail.

Chapter Eight
Whistles and Wharfs

Click, click, click. It was the sound of the door opening and it sent the two cats scurrying under the Captain's bunk. They watched a person walk back and forth from one end of the little room to the other, and felt him sit heavily on the edge of the bunk, causing the mattress to sag, just touching the tip of Chippiepierre's ears. They didn't move. They couldn't risk being seen. There was more movement in the mattress, and then a loud snoring noise filled the room.

"Who is that?" whispered Gidgett. "What should we do?"

"Shhhh, I think it's the Captain. We'll just have to be patient and wait him out. Let's try to get some sleep and hope Captain Tom finds some painting supplies."

"I thought Captain Tom was the Captain of this ship," whispered Gidgett.

"Apparently Captain Tom is a co-captain and helps take care of the ship and all things related to cats."

"Just try to stay quiet and get some sleep."

"Chippie? I hope you can paint us home by tomorrow night. I don't want to go to Baltimore."

"I don't want you to go there either, Gidgett. Now let's try to get some rest. Tomorrow will be a busy day if Captain Tom is successful in finding some painting supplies."

Unknown to the ship's Captain, the two cats slept beneath him. The Captain stirred when he heard the small cat door open, and Captain Tom came through.

"Hey Tom," said the Captain. "You're out kind of late tonight aren't you?" The Captain reached down and gently picked up the red tabby, placing him by his side, stroking him around his chin and ears.

"You must have had a busy day Tom; I didn't see you around the ship to-day at all." Captain Tom purred loudly as he settled in next to his Cap-tain.

"You have no idea the day I've had," thought Cap-tain Tom, all the while hoping that his new friends were well hidden. Then he fell into a deep sleep.

DING-DING...DING-DING...DING-DING...DING-DING. The ship's clock next to the Captain's bed was ringing. The alarm startled both cats. Chippiepierre banged his head on the sagging mattress and bunk frame.

"Ouch" cried Chippiepierre in a hushed tone. As he woke up, the reality of their situation filled him with dread. The two cats watched the Captain from his ankles down make his way around the room getting dressed. Chippiepierre prided himself on knowing shoes. At home he knew that workmen wore boots, and when he heard or saw boots he always thought it best to head to the basement. From what Chippiepieere could see, the captain wore a nice pair of polished black shoes. His pants, at least from the ankles down, were black with a crisp crease.

"The Captain is a nice dresser," whispered Chippiepierre.

At that moment, a brass button dropped on the floor and rolled toward the bunk. The two cats froze. Chippiepierre could see what was about to happen. This was it. Gidgett was going to bat at the button, and the Captain was going to reach down and find them hiding, right there under his bed. Chippiepierre quickly tried to imagine the punishment that would be given to two stowaway cats. But the button stopped rolling, and Gidgett resisted the urge to reach her paw out. Instead, the Captain stooped down and picked it up, never looking underneath.

"Are you sleeping in today Tom?" the Captain asked the big red tabby, who was still curled up on the bed. "I'll leave your food here for later. See you tonight."

The door shut with a clunk and the cats listened to the Captain's footsteps fading with distance.

"Phewww, that was a close call," said Chippiepierre.

"Frenchy, Gidgett, where are you?"

The two cats scampered out from under the bed and jumped up with Captain Tom.

"At home we always sleep with our people just like you slept with the Captain last night. I sleep in the middle, and Chippiepierre sleeps near the end of the bed. Your Captain seems very nice," said Gidgett, as she gently kneaded the soft bedding with her toes.

"He is very kind, and I got lucky. He rescued me from a wharf years ago, and ever since, he and I run this ship together."

"Chippiepierre and I were also rescued by our people. I was abandoned when I was just a tiny kitten. Chippiepierre was adopted from an animal shelter. So we got lucky, too."

"Gidgett, Captain Tom, I hate to break up such lovely conversation, but we need to focus on our objective. Were you able to find any paint supplies?" asked Chippiepierre.

"Yes, down in the ship's hold, but first let's share this breakfast." His words still lingered in the air as Chippiepierre and Gidgett gobbled down a good portion of Captain Tom's breakfast.

"Go ahead and finish it off. I'll get something down in the galley later." It was the first substantial meal the two had eaten since coming on board the ship and they wanted to savor every bite. Chippiepierre, however, couldn't enjoy the meal. He was worried about making another trip, unseen, down to the ship's hold. Plus, he knew he would have to paint the most important painting ever. Getting home safely depended on it.

"Okay you two, we better shove off before all the passengers are out strolling on the decks," said Captain Tom. The three cats exited through Captain Tom's official door and peered over the railing. Chippiepierre sniffed at the strange smells that hung in the air. It was a mixture of salty bay air and smoke from the huge smoke stack, plus a hint of breakfast from the dining room below. The splashing, whooshing sound of the side-wheels hummed in the background as the cats went down one flight of stairs in single file, with Captain Tom leading the way.

WHOOOOO WE WHOOOOOO, a loud steam whistle pierced the quiet morning.

At once, Gidgett and Chippiepierre slumped onto their bellies, wishing they could drop right through the deck.

"What's happening?" shouted Chippiepierre as the whistle sounded again.

"That? It's just the ship's whistle; we're approaching a wharf. We'd better stand out of the way. This ship gets very busy when we come into a wharf." Gidgett was paralyzed with fear. Her tail was at least three times its normally large size.

"That's some tail you have, Gidgett. You had better stow it away. One large breeze and it would act like a sail and blow you off the deck," joked Captain Tom.

The three friends moved into a shadow behind a deck chair and watched the ship came to life as the boat docked. People swarmed all around. Some were moving towards the railing to view the wharf. Others were gathering their belongings and preparing to go ashore. Dock mates handled enormous lines to tie up the ship. On shore, there were horse drawn carriages dropping people at the dock and taking

those that just got off the ship to other places. Farm animals were being brought on board as well as huge crates, barrels and steamer trunks. Chippiepierre and Gidgett watched in wonder.

"Look at all the people getting on and off this ship," said Chippiepierre. "Where are they going?"

"Well, some are going to Baltimore. Others will get off at stops along the way. There are hundreds of wharfs and many steamboats that serve the western side of Chesapeake Bay, where you are from, as well as the eastern shore of the bay. Towns on the eastern shore include places like Cape Charles, Tolchester Beach and a lot of stops in the Little Choptank River. But the City of Baltimore is the main port of call," explained Captain Tom.

"What will the people do in Baltimore?" asked Chippiepierre .

"Well, it's a big city, so they will do all kinds of things. Some are bringing their crops to be sold. Others may be visiting family, shopping or going to the doctor. In fact, some of the animals being brought on board are probably going to the veterinarian."

"Imagine that, going to the veterinarian by boat. It's bad enough going by car," said Chippiepierre.

"Where we come from, people go places in cars, not on ships or in carriages pulled by horses," said Gidgett, as she watched all the commotion below.

"Cars, what are cars?" asked Captain Tom.

"People drive them. They are like a carriage without a horse. They are powered by a small engine fueled by gasoline, not coal or steam," explained Chippiepierre.

"There are all kinds. Big, small, and even some that can carry many people at once. They're called buses and trucks. I've even heard our people talking about cars that are powered by electricity."

"Hmmm," murmured Captain Tom. "You don't use horses and carriages for transportation? How fast do these cars go?"

"They can go very fast, sixty miles per hour or more. At least, that's what I've heard my people say."

"That is fast!" exclaimed Captain Tom. "This ship generally travels about twelve miles per hour."

"We really have traveled back in time," said Chippiepierre, noting the differences between the world he was in now and the world they would need to get back to. He shuddered to think of the painting task ahead of him. "Will I really be able to paint our home so realistically that we will be able to go back through the painting?"

WHOOOOOO WE WHOOOOOO, the whistle blew, and this time startled Captain Tom, who was deep in thought trying to imagine a world with space satellites, electric lights, and cars where no one used horses or steamboats for transportation.

Soon the huge side wheels were sloshing and splashing through the water as the ship was getting underway. After pulling away from the wharf, the rhythm on the ship returned to normal, at least what Chippiepierre and Gidgett would call normal after more than twenty-four hours on board.

"Let's get down to the hold," said Captain Tom. "You've got to get working on the painting. It will have to be finished before we dock in Baltimore at two bells."

Chippiepierre and Gidgett looked puzzled.

"Oh, that's nine o'clock tonight," said Captain Tom. "I forgot, you don't know how to tell shipboard time."

Chapter Nine
A Beret and a Magic Tail

The three cats entered the ships hold and looked around. Tools of all shapes and sizes were secured along the walls, and there was not much light. In the corner were a number of cans of paint and some wood planks.

"There you go," said Captain Tom to Chippiepierre.

"Again with, "there you go?" What's that supposed to mean?"

"It means that there is some paint and some wood over there and that you should get working on your "masterpiece". I'm sorry, but this is a ship,

not an artists' studio. You'll have to work with the materials that are here."

Chippiepierre knew that Captain Tom was right and that he just had to get started.

"Could you help me move that wood plank and prop it up against that shelf? Then we need to place all the paint cans next to the plank where I can reach them." The three cats worked to set up a painting space spreading a cloth on the floor and opening the paint cans.

"It's awfully dark down here to work," murmured Chippiepierre, as he studied the colors of paint he had to work with. "Let's see, blue, yellow, red, and white. With these I should be able to mix any color paint I need." Slowly he dipped the tip of his tail in some blue paint, followed by some red, and then some white."

"That beret on your head is becoming bigger again, and there goes your tail. Look Captain Tom! Look at his tail. The tip is forming into a paintbrush! Be careful, don't make the house too blue. It's grayer than that."

"That hat or whatever you call it on your head is bigger. And I'll be, your tail does indeed look like a fine-tipped paintbrush," said a surprised Captain Tom, as he watched Chippiepierre applying the paint to the wood plank.

"The small tip is helpful for painting in the fine details. Now, I will need you both to be quiet while I am working."

"OOOKAYYYYYYYY, but I still think the house is too blue." whispered Gidgett, just barely loud enough to be heard.

Captain Tom could read Chippiepierre's exasperated expression, "Come on Gidgett, let's go find a little snack and let the artist work. There isn't much time before we will be in Baltimore."

Chippiepierre didn't even hear them leave. He was deep in concentration. Hours passed as he layered on the paint, at times blending the paints to achieve the desired color. Before moving to a different color or another part of the painting he carefully wiped his tail on the drop cloth.

"The house is not that exposed from the water. There are a lot more trees that I need to add. Let's see, yellow and blue make green," said Chippiepierre. As he worked, time passed.

"It's beautiful, it's our house!" exclaimed Gidgett as she came running into the ship's hold where Chippiepierre was working.

"When can we go home?" she asked.

"Not so fast. We have to be certain that this looks enough like our house, or we might not like where we would wind up."

"It looks good to me," said Gidgett as she paced anxiously around the painting.

"Something's not quite right, but I can't figure out what it is. Look carefully at the dock and see if you think everything is in the painting that would be on our dock at home."

"You painted in the crab pots; they look good. How about the yellow canoe? Should you paint that? I always like to crawl under it when our people are sitting down on the dock. Oh, and maybe you should paint in the green bench that they sit on."

"That's it! I knew I had forgotten something." Chippiepierre immediately went back to work adding in the yellow canoe and the green bench.

"Is that where you live?" asked Captain Tom as he stared at the painting. "You live on a dock?"

"No, you have to look carefully. The house is amongst the trees, in the background, up a slight slope, and the dock is in the foreground. My plan is to transport us to our dock, and then we will scamper up the slope to our house."

"Well Frenchy, I must say, that is some painting! How exactly do you propose to get into it?"

"Well, I am not exactly certain. Each time I've traveled into a painting it has happened differently. I don't have it down to an exact science, at least not yet."

"I don't imagine you do," said Captain Tom rolling his eyes.

"Captain Tom, do you want to come home with us?" asked Gidgett. "You would be welcome at our house. I would even share my favorite places with you. You would love the screen porch where we sit and watch the birds."

"Well," said Captain Tom, touched by the invitation. "I would like very much to see your home, but this ship is my home, and I would miss the Captain, and he would miss me, just as you miss your people."

"Oh," said Gidgett, realizing that Captain Tom would be as sad at their house, as she was on his ship.

"Ohhh Chippiepierre, PLEASE, can we go home now?" pleaded Gidgett.

As the three sat there looking at the painting the ship began to rock and pitch even more than it had in yesterday's storm.

"I knew we were expecting some rough weather, but I didn't think it would be coming in this early." said Captain Tom.

Now the ship was rocking and items in the hold were shifting. The water was splashing violently against the ship's hull, and it creaked and groaned.

"This is not a safe place to be in rough weather," shouted Captain Tom in order to be heard over the laboring engine, shifting cargo and howling wind. "We had better find a safer place to wait out this storm. Follow me!" As he turned back to make sure his friends were following him he saw the painting teetering back and forth; Chippiepierre and Gidgett were beneath it looking up.

"We can't leave the painting!" shouted Chippiepierre. "We have to bring it with us. There won't be enough time to paint another."

"There's no time! We can't carry it now!" shouted Captain Tom.
The painting was leaning over, and then…
"LOOK OUT!" shouted Captain Tom.

Chapter Ten
"Ahoy There, Captain Tom"

The sounds of ospreys filled the air, and the sun was warm on his black and white fur as he slowly lifted his aching head. He was very confused.

"Gidgett, where are you?"

"Gidgett, are you here? Are you alright?"

There was no answer.

"Maybe she isn't here. In fact, where am I?"

"Purrrr-rrrr, Chip-piepierre it's dark. Where are you?"

"Gidgett, I hear you, but I don't see you."

Then Chippiepierre managed to turn his aching head and he saw a gigantic black fluffy tail sticking out from under the yellow canoe.

"Gidgett! It's dark because your head is under the yellow canoe! We're home!"

"We're home! We're home!" shouted Gidgett as she crawled out of the dark.

"Look! Through the trees! There's our house!"

Just then, they heard their names being called CHIPPPPIEE, GII-IDDDGETTT, CHIIIPPPPEEEE, GIIIDETTTT, and the sound of a spoon tapping on a can of cat food calling them in.

The two looked at each other and raced up the path. They jumped up

in a single bound onto the deck and into the house. Their smiling people followed them closely.

After lots of petting, lap time with their people and plenty of food, Chippiepierre and Gidgett went upstairs and settled onto the window seat overlooking their yard.

They were exhausted. They cuddled together in a tight ball. The black and white of their fur all blended together. They didn't need to say much.

"Chippiepierre, are you awake? Do you think it was all just a bad dream?"

"I don't know Gidgett," replied Chippiepierre. "It would be weird for us to both have the same dream."

"I don't think you should ever touch those paints again."

"You are probably right. But I love the paints, the smells, the brushes, and blending. I'll just be more careful from now on. I'll be real careful." Gidgett was too tired to argue any further, and she drifted off to sleep next to her best friend.

The following morning when everyone in the house was asleep, Chippiepierre bounded down the basement steps two at a time. The familiar smell of paints filled the air.

"I just have to see what happened to the steamboat painting after it crashed," said Chippiepierre. Very cautiously he approached the painting table and jumped up. Stepping lightly around paints, palettes, and jars of brushes he approached the painting on the easel.

"Imagine that, the painting isn't damaged. At least I won't get in trouble." Chippiepierre was astonished and greatly relieved.

"It's amazing that it didn't tear or break when it fell on the floor." Chippiepierre moved in for a closer examination of the painting, noticing some long and short black and white fur stuck on the canvas. As he looked the painting over, the old steamboat was now very familiar to him. He recognized the decks, and lifeboats, he could hear the splashing of the huge sidewheels churning through the water and see the huge walking beam moving up and down. He could smell the soot from the coal furnace. As he looked at the Captain's quarters attached to the rounded pilot house he saw something that he didn't remember seeing in the painting before it had crashed to the floor. Chippiepierre blinked his eyes, shook his head and blinked again.

"It can't be; it must be magic," thought Chippiepierre, moving closer to the painting until his whiskers touched the canvas. Sure enough, it was a red and white striped tabby cat with more stripes than he had ever seen before. Chippiepierre stared at the painting for a very long time in disbelief trying to make sense out of his and Gidgett's adventure.

"Ahoy there, Captain Tom," he said very softly, still staring at the painting.

As Chippiepierre turned to jump down, he heard a familiar voice. He turned back towards the painting and was certain he heard Captain Tom say, "Well done, Frenchy."

THE END

Glossary
Words You Might Might Want To Know

Beret: a soft round cap or hat with no visor, commonly worn in France.

Easel: a wooden triangular frame that supports an artist's canvas.

Galley: the kitchen where food is prepared on a ship.

Hurricane Deck: the top deck on a passenger steamer.

Ship Board Time: timekeeping on board a ship that signified the crew's change of watch at 12:00, 4:00 and 8:00; bells chimed every half hour repeating in 4 hour increments.

Sir Isaac Newton: an English scientist who lived from 1642 to 1727 who framed many universal laws of physics, notably gravity.

Stevedores: men who worked on the docks loading and unloading cargo.

Stowaway: someone who secretly boards a ship without buying a ticket and hides to avoid being detected.

Walking Beam: the large mechanical diamond shaped structure that was connected to the steam-driven pistons and the crankshaft to the large paddlewheel which powered the ship through the water.

Wharf: the landings along the bay and rivers where the steamboats would dock and pick up or discharge passengers and cargo.

Fun Facts
Did You Know?

1. Walking Beams could weigh on average about 15 tons (about the weight of 7 cars).

2. The steamboat Lancaster was built in 1892. It had accommodations for 80 first-class passengers and 97 second-class passengers. There were 42 crew members.

3. The steamboat Lancaster was 205 feet long by 56 feet wide. Each side-wheel was 30 feet high.

4. In 1911 the steamboat "Neuse" outfitted with the newest propeller technology, raced the steamboat Lancaster from Smith Point Virginia, to Baltimore Harbor. The race lasted six hours. The Lancaster, with her side-wheels won the race by 10 minutes.

5. Tomatoes were formerly a major crop in the tidewater region. During tomato canning season the waters in the creeks would often run red from the canning process.

6. It is believed that about 150 steamboats sank in the Chesapeake Bay.

7. The cost of a ticket, one-way from Baltimore to Fredericksburg was about $8.00

8. The Captain in the pilot house would communicate with the engine room with a series of bells.

9. In 1895 the Smith Point lighthouse was damaged by ice flows. The Lighthouse keepers had to escape onto the ice before the lighthouse was swept away.

10. In 1933 a major hurricane damaged many of the wharfs along the steamboat routes. The loss of wharfs, plus the use of vehicles and improved roads led to the end of the use of steamboats as the method of transportation in the tidewater region.

Research Sources and References
Learning More

1. Burgess, Robert H., *This was Chesapeake Bay*, (Centreville, MD: Tidewater Publishers, 1994)

2. Burgess, Robert H. and Wood, H. Graham, *Steamboats Out Of Baltimore*, (Cambridge, MD: Tidewater Publishers, 1968)

3. Holly, David C., *Chesapeake Steamboats: Vanished Fleet* (Centreville, MD: Tidewater Publishers, 1994)

4. Holly, David C., *Steamboat on the Chesapeake: Emma Giles and the Tolchester Line* (Centreville, MD: Tidewater Publishers, 1987)

5. Holly, David C., *Tidewater By Steamboat: A Saga of the Chesapeake* (Baltimore, MD: The Johns Hopkins University Press, 2000)

6. The Reedville Fisherman's Museum, Reedville Virginia

7. The Steamboat Era Museum, Irvington Virginia

8. United States Lighthouse Society, Chesapeake Chapter (Internet Reference) <http://www.cheslights.org/cheskids/html/type-lights.htm

Acknowledgments

I have many to thank for their help along the way, as I envisioned and wrote this book. First and foremost, I thank my husband, Richard Kantor, for his encouragement and enthusiasm, his insightful editing and the use of his painting of the Steamboat Lancaster. He always knew there would be a book, even when I had my doubts.

Also, special thanks go to my friend, and the illustrator of this book, George Frayne. Our shared interest of the Steamboat Era, brought us together. He embraced the concept of the story, and his detailed and fanciful illustrations have brilliantly captured the essence of the characters and life on the steamboat.

Other acknowledgements go to; the Rappatomac Writers group for listening, critiquing and suggesting; Janet Abbott Fast for encouraging me to stick to my story; My friend Fred Kelsey, he was consultant on all things nautical, specifically shipboard time; my walking buddies, Brenda Gilbert and Ruth Fast, they both logged many miles with me as my story unfolded; my Animal Welfare League friends for their support and enthusiasm; Suzanne Mattingly for her encouragement throughout, and computer help on a specific Sunday afternoon; Mariann Smith Disney for her encouragement and interest in the project; my niece Hailey Dietz for providing a ten year olds point of view; Terri Thaxton and Anne McClintock of the Steamboat Era Museum, in Irvington, VA; volunteers from the Reedville Fisherman's Museum, in Reedville, VA; Tonya Carter, Children's Librarian of the Lancaster Community Library; Julianne Bates, Children's Librarian of the Northumberland Public Library; Narielle Living for her editing suggestions; and Tom Crockett for his assistance in the production of this book.

About the Author
Barbara Dietz

Barbara Dietz was born and raised on the New Jersey Shore and has fond memories of bicycling to the beach and riding waves all summer. She attended Stockton State College, earning a degree in Environmental Studies and Fairleigh Dickinson University, where she earned a Masters' degree. She enjoyed a career with the New Jersey Department of Environmental Protection before retiring and moving to Virginia's Northern Neck.

The history of the Chesapeake Bay Steamboats and their significance to Virginia's tidewater region inspired Barb to write *Chippiepierre's Magic Paintbrush Tail: A Steamboat Adventure*. She lives in Merry Point Virginia with her husband, artist, Richard Kantor. It is his oil painting of the Steamboat Lancaster that is featured on the book's cover. They share their home with their two cats, Chippiepierre and Gidgett. Barb enjoys traveling, rock hounding, and nature and is passionate about animal welfare. She is a volunteer with the Animal Welfare League of the Northern Neck. Barb is a member of the Chesapeake Bay Writers and the Society of Children's Book Writers and Illustrators.

About the Illustrator
George Frayne

George Frayne is an accomplished graphic designer, illustrator, and filmmaker. He attended Pratt Institute and New York University. During World War II he served in Europe as a bomber pilot in the United States Army Air Force. He was involved in advertising artwork and documentary film production for many years in New York, and was a Curator at the Long Island Maritime Museum. After moving to Virginia's Northern Neck, he served as the Director and Curator for the Reedville Fishermen's Museum and as the Exhibition Designer for the Steamboat Era Museum in Irvington, Virginia. George resides in Reedville, Virginia, and is currently working on new design projects.

George Frayne and Barbara Dietz

Made in the USA
Charleston, SC
16 November 2013